MW00398795

DUNDER
MIFFLIN INC
PAPER COMPANY

1725 SLOUGH AVENUE
SCRANTON, PA 18505

the office

Antics and Adventures
from Dunder Mifflin

RP MINIS

PHILADELPHIA

RP Minis™
Hachette Book Group
1290 Avenue of the Americas, New York, NY 10104
www.runningpress.com
@Running_Press

Printed in China

First Edition: April 2020

Published by RP Minis, an imprint of Perseus Books, LLC, a subsidiary of Hachette Book Group, Inc. The RP Minis name and logo is a trademark of the Hachette Book Group.

The publisher is not responsible for websites (or their content) that are not owned by the publisher.

Library of Congress Control Number: 2019949763

ISBN: 978-0-7624-9835-2

LREX

10 9 8 7 6 5 4 3 2 1

CONTENTS

Introduction

With its incredibly quotable lines and unforgettable cast of characters, *The Office* takes the title as one of the most popular comedy series of all time, running for a total of nine seasons and racking up 42 Emmy nominations along the way. The beloved show follows the lives of a group of eccentric, lovable employees working monotonous middle America jobs for a Scranton, Pennsylvania, paper company called Dunder Mifflin.

There's Michael Scott, regional sales manager, who continually sticks his foot in his mouth; Dwight Schrute, the assistant (to the) regional manager, who may lack social skills but is rolling in beets;

Jim and Pam, star-crossed lovers who regularly team up to play pranks on Dwight; Ryan, a grown-up Frat boy; Angela, a type-A cat lady; Phyllis, a sweet yet kind of odd woman; Kelly, the narcissistic chatterbox; Creed, the creepy guy; Oscar, the voice of reason; Kevin, the lovable buffoon; Stanley, gloomy but nearly retired; Andy, the Cornell grad; Toby, the divorced dad; Erin, Pam's positive and sweet replacement; Gabe, the go-to scapegoat; Darryl, the ambitious assistant warehouse manager; and Meredith, the resident nymphomaniac alcoholic.

On the pages that follow, you'll fall in love all over again with the quirky staff of Dunder Mifflin, relive some of the show's most hilarious and memorable moments, and learn a few life lessons along the way.

Things You Should Never Say at the Office

Darryl:

"I wanted to leave quietly,
it seemed dignified. But
having Kevin grind up on
my front, while Erin pretended
to hump me from behind,
it was a more accurate tribute
to my years here. I'm gonna
miss these guys."

Michael:

"Toby works in HR, which technically means he works for corporate, so he's really not a part of our family. Also, he's divorced, so he's really not a part of his family."

Stanley:

∙∙∙∙∙∙∙∙∙∙∙∙∙∙∙∙∙∙∙∙∙∙∙∙∙∙∙∙∙

"I do not like pregnant women in my workspace. They're always complaining. I have varicose veins, too. I have swollen ankles. I'm constantly hungry. Do you think my nipples don't get sore, too? Do you think I don't need to know the fastest way to the hospital?"

Michael:

"There's no such thing as an inappropriate joke. That's why it's called a joke."

Dunder Mifflin Duds

Ryan:

• •

"I miss the days when there
was only one party I didn't
want to go to."

Stanley:

"It's true. Around this office in the past I have been a little abrupt with people. The doctor said if I can't find a new way to relate more positively to my surroundings, I'm going to die. I'm going to die."

Toby:

"This morning I saw a little bird fly into the glass doors downstairs and die. And I had to keep going."

Michael:

"Well, happy birthday, Jesus. Sorry your party's so lame."

Stanley:

"I wake up every morning to a bed that's too small. Drive my daughter to a school that's too expensive. And then I go to work for a job in which I get paid too little. But on Pretzel Day? Well, I like Pretzel Day."

Kevin:

"Mini cupcakes? As in the mini version of regular cupcakes? Which is already a mini version of a cake? Honestly, where does it end with you people?"

**Moments of Clarity
vs. Insanity**

Kelly:

"I am one of the few people who looks hot eating a cupcake."

Michael:

....

"I have flaws. What are they? I sing in the shower. Sometimes I spend too much time volunteering. Occasionally I'll hit somebody with my car."

Jim:

"Today, I am meeting a potential client on the golf course because Ryan put me on probation. You remember Ryan: he was the temp here. It is not a good time for me to lose my job since I have some pretty big long-term plans in my personal life with Pam that I'd like her parents to be psyched about. So, I am about to do something very bold in this job that I've never done before: try."

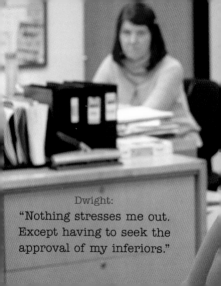

Dwight:

"Nothing stresses me out.
Except having to seek the
approval of my inferiors."

Kelly:
"I talk a lot, so I've
learned to just tune
myself out."

Michael:

················

"I'm an early bird
and I'm a night owl.
So, I'm wise and I
have worms."

Kevin:

"I have very little patience for stupidity."

Michael:

··

"I love inside jokes.
I'd love to be part
of one someday."

Darryl:
"Seems like the better title I have, the stupider my job gets."

· ·

"Right now, this is just a
job. If I advance any higher
in this company, this would
be my career. And, uh, if
this were my career, I'd
have to throw myself in
front of a train."

"Do I need to be liked?
Absolutely not. I like to
be liked. I enjoy being
liked. I have to be liked.
But it's not like this
compulsive need to
be liked, like my need
to be praised."

Dwight:

"There's too many
people on this earth.
We need a new plague."

Co-Worker Musings

Creed:

"A lot of jazz cats are blind. But, they can play the piano like nobody's business. I'd like to put the piano in front of Pam without her glasses and see what happens. I'd also like to see her topless."

Pam:

"Once every hour, someone is involved in an internet scam. That man is Michael Scott. He's supporting about twenty Nigerian princesses."

Jim: "Stanley just drank OJ out of my mug and didn't seem to realize that it wasn't his hot coffee. So the question has to be asked, is there no limit to what he won't notice?"

Andy:

"Not only is Erin really
sweet and cute, she smells
like my mom."

Romance
at the Office

Dwight:

"Women are like wolves.
If you want one you must
trap it. Snare it. Tame it.
Feed it."

"When you're a kid, you assume your parents are soul mates. My kids are gonna be right about that."

Creed: "So, hey, I want to set you up with my daughter."

Jim: "Oh, I'm engaged to Pam."

Creed: "I thought you were gay."

Jim: "Then why would you want to set me up with your daughter?"

Kelly:

"You want to call
someone that texted
you? Do you want to
drive them away?"

"Reject a woman and she will never let it go. One of the many defects of their kind. Also, weak arms."

Erin:

"Thank God he's my boss, because I would not have said yes to a first date if I didn't have to."

Overheard
at the Office

Creed:

"You know, a human can go
on living for several hours
after being decapitated."

Dwight:

"You're thinking of a chicken."

Creed:

"What did I say?"

Kelly:
"I don't talk trash,
I talk smack.
They're totally
different."

Erin: "Do you want me to spin you in your chair and make you dizzy?"

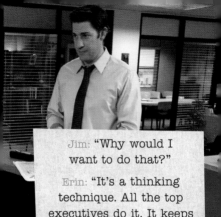

Jim: "Why would I want to do that?"

Erin: "It's a thinking technique. All the top executives do it. It keeps the brain moving, and a spinning brain is a working brain."

Creed:

"Nobody steals from Creed Bratton and gets away with it. The last person to do this disappeared. His name? Creed Bratton."

Kelly: "Well, I manage my department, and I've been doing that for several years now. And, God, I've learned a lot of life lessons along the way."

Jim: "Your department's just you, right?"

Kelly: "Yes, Jim, but I am not easy to manage."

"I'm not Rumpelstiltskin,
Jim, I can't keep spinning
gold out of your s—t."

Schrute Smarts

Dwight:

"I don't have a lot of experience with vampires, but I have hunted werewolves. I shot one once, but by the time I got to it, it had turned back into my neighbor's dog."

· ·

"I am faster than
80 percent of
all snakes."

Dwight:

"Why tip someone for a job I'm capable of doing myself? I can deliver food. I can drive a taxi. I can, and do, cut my own hair. I did, however, tip my urologist, because I am unable to pulverize my kidney stones."

Dwight:

"I grew up on a farm.
I have seen animals
having sex in every
position imaginable.
Goat on chicken.
Chicken on goat.
Couple of chickens
doing a goat, couple
of pigs watching."

Dwight:

"If I could menstruate, I wouldn't have to deal with idiotic calendars anymore. I'd just be able to count down from my previous cycle. Plus, I'd be more in tune with the moon and tides."

Dwight:

"When my mother was pregnant with me, they did an ultrasound and found she was having twins. When they did another ultrasound a few weeks later, they discovered that I had absorbed the other fetus. Do I regret this? No, I believe his tissue has made me stronger. I now have the strength of a grown man and a little baby."

Dwight:

"I never smile if I can help it. Showing one's teeth is a submission signal in primates. When someone smiles at me, all I see is a chimpanzee begging for its life."

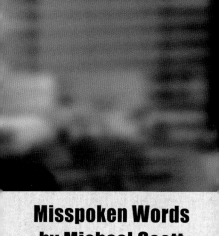

Misspoken Words
by Michael Scott

"I'm not superstitious, but I'm a little stituous."

Michael:

"Fool me once,
strike one.
Fool me twice,
strike three."

Michael:

"Tell him to call me
ASAP as possible."

Michael:

"Well, well, well, how the turntables . . . "

That's What She Said

Phyllis:

"We have a gym
at home.
It's called
the bedroom."

Oscar:

"If you would
have seen the
look he gave me,
he wanted to rock
more than just
my vote."

Michael:
"I want you to think
about it long and hard."

Dwight:
"That's what she said."

Michael:
"Don't. Don't you dare."

"I've had two men fight over me before. Usually it's over which one gets to hold the camcorder."

Darryl:

"You need to get back on top."

Michael:

"That's what she said."

Gabe:

"Michael, you're making this harder than it has to be."

Michael:

"That's what she said."

**Shockingly
Sound Advice**

"Before I do anything
I ask myself, 'Would
an idiot do that?'
And if the answer
is yes, I do not do
that thing."

Pam:

"There's a lot of beauty in ordinary things. Isn't that kind of the point?"

Meredith:

"Like my mom
always says:
Talk classy,
act nasty."

Phyllis:

"Close your
mouth, sweetie.
You look like
a trout."

"I've been involved in a number of cults, both as a leader and a follower. You have more fun as a follower, but you make more money as a leader."

Dwight:

"You only live once?
False. You live every day.
You only die once."

Pam:

"Be strong. Trust yourself. Love yourself. Conquer your fears. Just go after what you want and act fast, because life just isn't that long."

"I'll be the number-two
guy here in Scranton in
six weeks. How? Name
repetition, personality
mirroring, and never
breaking off a handshake.
I'm always thinking
one step ahead. Like a . . .
carpenter . . . that
makes stairs."

Stanley:

"Life is short. Drive fast and leave a sexy corpse. That's one of my mottos."